W9-APN-808

# I AM NOT A CHAIR!

Ross Burach

HARPER
*An Imprint of* HarperCollins*Publishers*

**FOR DREW AND TODD**

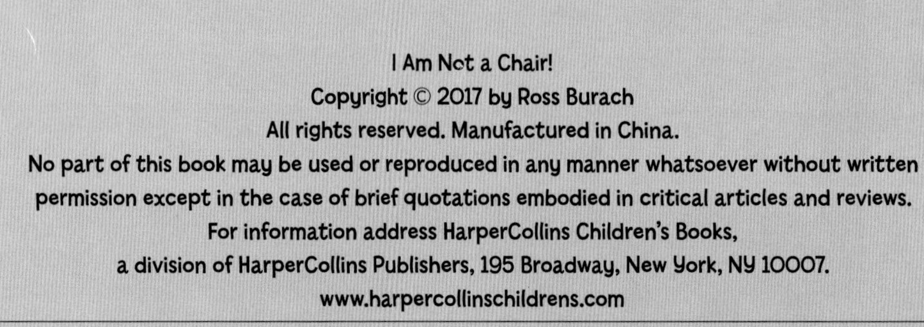

I Am Not a Chair!



For information address HarperCollins Children's Books,
a division of HarperCollins Publishers, 195 Broadway, New York, NY 10007.
www.harpercollinschildrens.com

ISBN 978-0-06-236016-8

The artist used pencil and acrylic paints colored digitally to create the illustrations for this book.

Typography by Chelsea C. Donaldson

16 17 18 19 20 SCP 10 9 8 7 6 5 4 3 2 1

❖

First Edition

On Giraffe's first day in the jungle . . .

he felt something wasn't right.

Can I share
that chair?
ABC
ABC

**CHAIR?**

**I AM NOT A CHAIR!**

Giraffe knew he needed
to clear things up right away . . .

but . . .
SPLAT!

. . . he couldn't get the words out.

I'm a giraffe. Can't they see?

I have

**SPOTS**

and

**EARS**

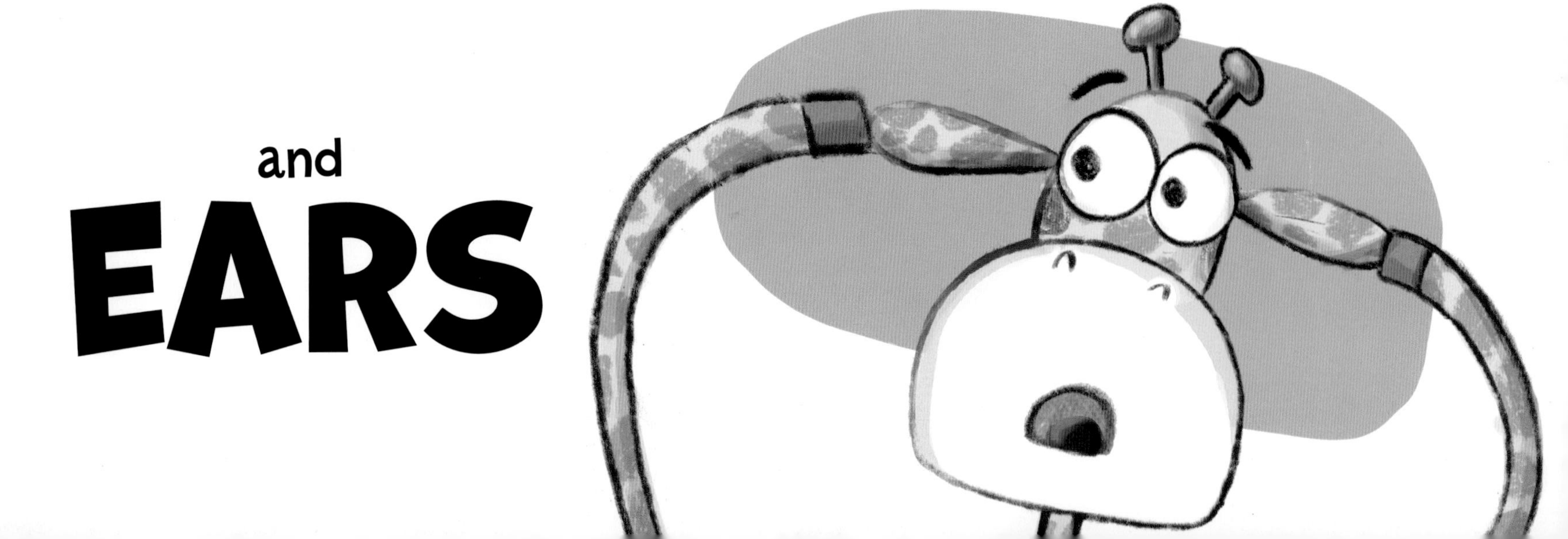

and **EYES**

and whatever

**THESE**

things are. . . .

If they couldn't SEE the difference,
Giraffe would have to SHOW them.

TWIST
TWIST
KLANK
CLONK

Now, THAT'S a chair.
Looks nothing like me!

New friends were already
headed his way! Problem solved.

OOOOMPH!
WOBBLE
WOBBLE
WOBBLE

SMASH!
Oh no!
My chair!

I'll fix it!
SNIFF
SNIFF
This goes here.
That goes there.

Giraffe's first day could not get any worse.
But at least no one could sit on him now.

FLAP
FLAP
FLAP

While Giraffe looked for a solution,
someone was spying on him. . . .

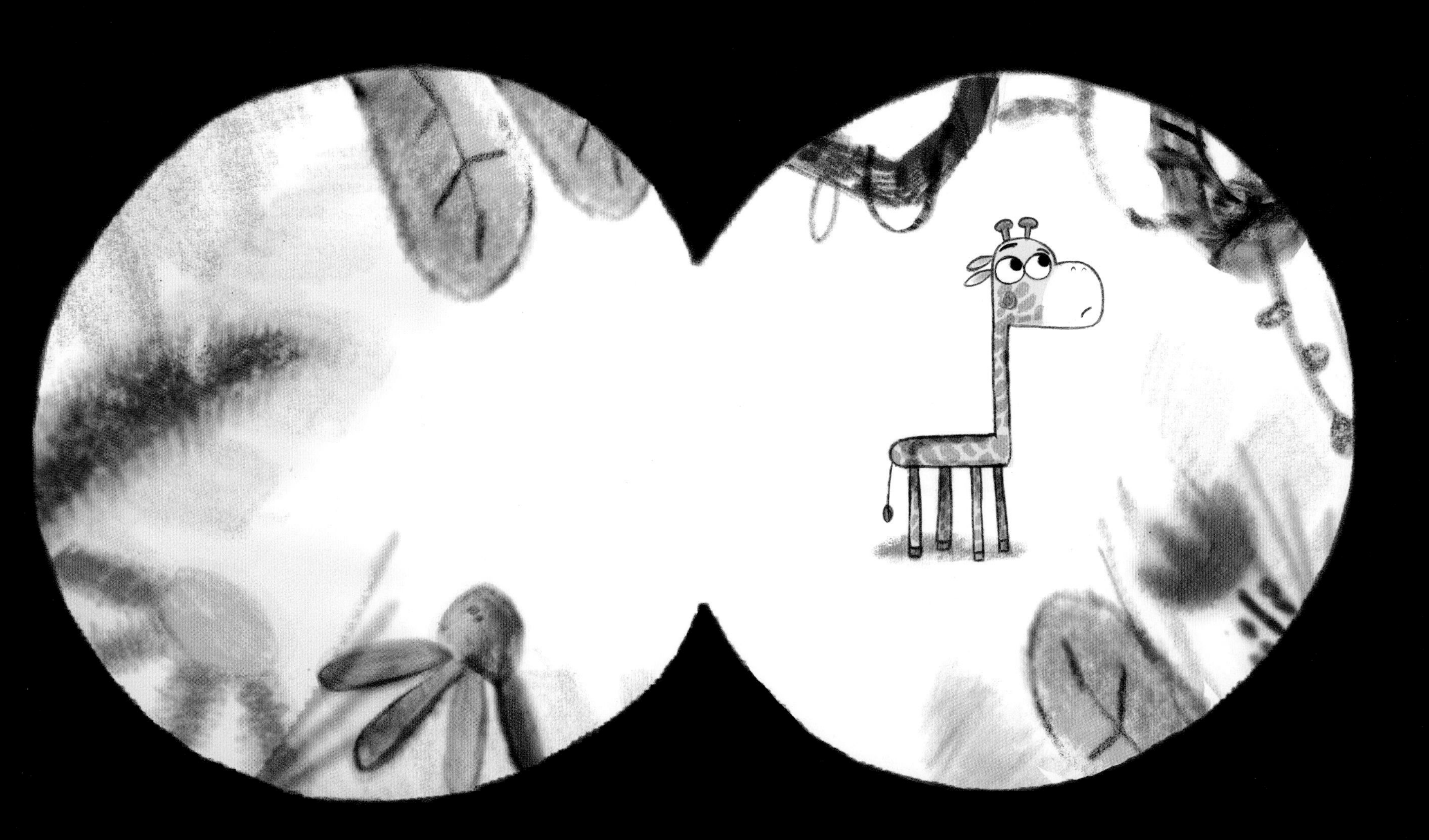

A HUMAN!
Surely he'll know who I am.

It's perfect!

Ahhhh.
click

Z Z Z Z Z Z Z Z
Smartest species?
Yeah, right.

# EEEEEENOUGH!!

# I. AM. NOT. A. CHAIR!

And I'm speaking up to the NEXT ANIMAL I SEE.

ROAR

The next animal I see . . .
WILL—BE—MY
DINNER!

Even if I have to sit here

# ALL NIGHT!

Giraffe wished he could run.
He wished he could hide.
He wished he wasn't so afraid.

Giraffe couldn't hold it in any longer. . . .

I'VE GOT TO
PEE!

Okay, here goes nothing.
GULP

E-e-excuse me.

AHHHHH!
RUN FOR YOUR LIVES!!!
A TALKING CHAIR!!!

I am not a chair.
I am a GIRAFFE.

And the next day,
he told everyone!

And everything felt right.

Me! A chair.
Can you believe it?